For Sam – JE

For Tilly – CF

MYRIAD BOOKS LIMITED
35 Bishopsthorpe Road, London SE26 4PA

First published in 2005 by
PICCADILLY PRESS LIMITED
5 Castle Road, London NW1 8PR
www.piccadillypress.co.uk

Text copyright © Joseph Ellis, 2005
Illustrations copyright © Christyan Fox, 2005

ISBN 1 84746 117 4
EAN 9 781847 461179

Designed by Christyan Fox

Printed in China

One Clever Creature

Joseph Ellis and Christyan Fox

MYRIAD BOOKS LIMITED

All around the
world, animals do
AMAZING things.

Some can
swim,

others can fly,

some can dig deep

or jump really high.

But...

Goats can't paint pictures.

Frogs can't give hugs.

Hippos can't wave.

Can polar bears sing a song?

Can a penguin
count to three?

A cat can't bang a drum.

A dog can't clap along.

Or a tortoise climbing up the stairs?

Can you imagine a hen in your bath, washing her feathers with your best bubbly soap,

or a fox brushing
his teeth
before bed?

An owl can't
read a book.

A bat can't kiss
goodnight.

But would you believe me if I said I know a clever creature who CAN do all these things?

Well, there is one,
it's true. And this
clever creature is...